THE STORY OF JESUS

Retold by Heather Amery
Illustrated by Norman Young

Language consultant: Betty Root
Series editor: Jenny Tyler

3 The Christmas Story
19 Jesus in the Temple
33 Jesus Calms the Storm
43 Jairus's Daughter
51 Loaves and Fishes
67 The Good Samaritan
83 The Easter Story

NOTES FOR PARENTS

These Bible stories have been written in such a way that young children can succeed in their first attempts to read.

To help achieve this success, first read the whole story aloud to your child and talk about the pictures. Then encourage your child to read the short, simple text at the top of each page, and read the longer text at the bottom of the page yourself. Taking turns with reading builds up a child's confidence and provides the additional fun of joining in. It is a great day when children discover that they can read a whole story for themselves.

Bible Tales provide an enjoyable opportunity for parents and children to share the excitement and satisfaction of learning to read.

Betty Root

The Christmas Story

This is Mary and Joseph.

They lived a long time ago in Nazareth. Joseph was a carpenter. Mary was expecting a baby soon.

Mary and Joseph had to walk most of the way.
They had to register to pay their taxes.

Bethlehem was full of people.

Mary and Joseph tried to find a room to sleep in. But everywhere was already full.

They stopped at the last inn.

“All my rooms are full,” said the innkeeper, “but you can sleep in the stable, if you like.”

The stable was warm and clean.

Joseph made a bed of straw for Mary. He covered it with his cloak. Mary lay down. She was very tired.

That night her baby son was born.

Mary called him Jesus. She put him in clean clothes and made a bed for him in a manger.

Near the town were some shepherds.

They slept near their sheep to guard them from wild animals. It was very quiet and dark that night.

Suddenly, there was a bright light.

The night sky was filled with light. The shepherds woke up with a start. They were very scared.

An angel spoke to them.

"Don't be afraid. Go to Bethlehem. In a stable, you will find a baby who is Christ the Lord."

The shepherds went to Bethlehem.

They soon found the stable and knelt in front of the baby. They told Mary what the angel had said.

The shepherds were very happy.

They told everyone in Bethlehem about Jesus.
Then they went back to their sheep, singing to God.

Far away were three Wise Men.

They saw a very bright star moving across the sky.
It meant something special had happened.

They followed the star.

After many days, it stopped over Bethlehem. The Wise Men knew they had come to the right place.

The Wise Men found Jesus.

They went in and saw Mary with her baby. They knelt down and gave the presents they had brought.

Mary and Joseph went home.

They took baby Jesus on a very long, hard journey. At last, they were back home in Nazareth.

Jesus in the Temple

This is Jesus.

He lived with his mother, Mary, and Joseph in Nazareth. He went to school there.

Mary and Joseph went to Jerusalem.

They went every year for a special Jewish festival.
When Jesus was twelve, he went with them.

It was a long journey.

Mary, Joseph and Jesus walked with lots of other families and friends. They camped each night.

At last, they arrived in Jerusalem.

They stayed in the city for several days. When the festival was over, they went home to Nazareth.

They camped for the first night.

“Where’s Jesus?” asked Mary. “He must be with another family,” said Joseph.

Jesus was missing.

Mary and Joseph searched all night for him. But they couldn't find Jesus anywhere.

Mary and Joseph packed up their things.

It was early in the morning. They hurried back to Jerusalem to look for Jesus.

"Where can Jesus be?" asked Mary.
They were very worried about Jesus. They searched all the streets for him but couldn't find him.

At last, they found Jesus.
"There he is," said Mary. He was sitting with the Temple teachers, listening to them talking.

Jesus surprised the teachers.

He asked them many questions. He was only twelve but he understood all their answers.

“Why did you go away?” asked Mary.

“We’ve been so worried about you. We’ve been looking everywhere for you,” she said.

"I'm sorry," said Jesus.
"Didn't you know I'd be in my Father's house."
Mary didn't understand what Jesus meant.

They went home to Nazareth.

Jesus grew up to be a wise and strong young man. He loved Mary and Joseph, and he loved God.

Jesus calms the Storm

This is Jesus.

He walked around the country with his twelve special friends. They were called his disciples.

Jesus talked to the people.

He told them they should love God and obey Him. Jesus made the ill people well again.

One evening, Jesus was tired.

He had talked to people all day. Jesus asked his disciples to take him across Lake Galilee.

Jesus got on a boat.

He lay down and was soon fast asleep. The disciples took the boat away across the lake.

Suddenly there was a great storm.

The wind blew and huge waves splashed into the boat. The disciples were very frightened.

A disciple woke Jesus up.

"Master," he shouted, "please save us. Can't you see we are going to drown?"

Jesus stood up in the boat.

He held up his arm. “Hush, be still,” he said. At once, the wind dropped and the water was calm.

"Why were you afraid?"
"Didn't you believe I'd look after you?" Jesus asked the disciples. They didn't know what to say.

The boat sailed on across Lake Galilee.

The sea was calm. The disciples wondered how Jesus could tell the wind and waves what to do.

Jairus's Daughter

One day a man ran up to Jesus.

His name was Jairus. “My child is very ill. Please come and make her better again,” he said.

Jesus went with Jairus.

A woman ran to meet them, crying. “You are too late. The little girl is dead,” she said.

"She is not dead," said Jesus.

"She is only asleep." Jesus walked to the house. He went in with three of his disciples.

"Everyone but the girl's mother and father, and my disciples, must leave the house," Jesus said.

Jesus held the girl's hand.

"Little girl, get up," said Jesus. At once the girl opened her eyes and got off her bed.

"She's alive," said Jairus.

The little girl's mother and father were surprised and very happy to see her alive and well.

"Give her some food," said Jesus.

Then Jesus and his three disciples left the house and went quietly on their way.

Loaves and Fishes

Jesus talked to the people.

Everywhere he went with his disciples, people in the towns and villages came to listen to him.

He told them that they should love God. And he taught them how they should pray to Him.

One day, Jesus sailed across the lake.

He and his disciples stopped at a quiet place on the shore. They climbed a hill and sat down to rest.

Soon lots of people came.

They heard Jesus was there. They came from the towns and villages until there was a huge crowd.

"Tell them to go home," said a disciple.

Jesus felt very sorry for the people. He talked to them, answered questions and made the ill ones well again.

"Now send them away."
"It's getting late and the people are hungry," said a disciple. "They have no food."

"We must feed them," said Jesus.

"Even a huge amount of money would not buy food for them all," said Philip, one of the disciples.

A small boy stood up.

He opened his bag. "Look, I have brought a picnic with me," he said to Andrew, another disciple.

“This boy has food.”

“He has five little bread rolls and two small fishes,” Andrew said to Jesus. “Not much for this huge crowd.”

“May I take your picnic?”

“Will you share it with us?” Jesus asked the boy.
“Yes, Master,” said the boy. “Thank you,” said Jesus.

Jesus took the food.

“Tell the people to sit down,” Jesus said to the disciples. There were about five thousand people.

Jesus held up the loaves and fishes.

He said a prayer of thanks to God. Then he broke up the food into pieces. “Give it to the people,” he said.

The disciples gave out the food.

The people sat down on the grass. The more food the disciples gave out, the more there seemed to be.

Everyone had enough to eat.

The disciples were very surprised. The five thousand people ate bread and fish until they were full.

Then the people went home.

“Collect up the leftover food,” said Jesus. His disciples filled twelve baskets and took them home.

The Good Samaritan

Jesus told the people stories.

A man said to him, "God says we must be kind to people. But which people?" Jesus told him this story.

There was a man who was a Jew.

He lived in Jerusalem. One day he started on a long journey to Jericho. He had to walk all the way.

He was alone.

He knew it was dangerous to go on his own. People usually went with other people because of robbers.

Suddenly he saw some robbers.

They ran up to him, shouting and waving sticks.
The man was frightened and tried to run away.

The robbers caught the man.

They beat him with their sticks. They knocked him down and kicked him while he lay on the ground.

They stole everything.

The robbers took most of the man’s clothes. They stole his money and his bag. Then they ran away.

The man was badly wounded.

He lay bleeding on the dusty ground. He was so badly hurt, he could not get up or call for help.

Soon a priest came by.
He looked at the wounded man, but he didn't stop.
He made his donkey hurry away down the road.

Then another man came along.
He worked in the temple in Jerusalem. He saw the man but he didn't stop. He hurried down the road.

Then a third man came along.

He was a Samaritan. Although the Samaritans and the Jews hated each other, this man stopped.

The Samaritan got off his donkey.

He poured oil on the man’s wounds to soothe them and wine to heal them. Then he bandaged them.

The Samaritan lifted the man onto his donkey. Then he led the donkey down the road to the city of Jericho.

The Samaritan put the man to bed for the night and made him comfortable. He bought him supper.

The Samaritan left the next morning.

He paid the innkeeper. “Look after this man,” he said. “I’ll pay any extra bills when I come this way again.”

“Which man was kind?” asked Jesus.

“The Samaritan,” said the man. “Yes,” said Jesus, “We should be kind to anyone who needs our help.”

The Easter Story

Jesus went to Jerusalem.

He rode into the great city of Jerusalem on a donkey. His twelve disciples walked along with him.

The people cheered Jesus.

They cut down palms and laid them on the road. They had heard he was their new leader.

That night Jesus had a special supper.
Jesus told his twelve disciples that he would die soon. Judas, one of the disciples, left the room.

Jesus broke up some bread.

He gave a piece to each disciple. "This is my body which I give for you," he said.

Jesus picked up a cup of wine.

"This is my blood. I give it for you and all people," he said. Each disciple drank wine from the cup.

Then Jesus went to a garden to pray.

Eleven disciples went with him. Judas had gone to tell the enemies of Jesus where to find him.

Soldiers came to arrest Jesus.

The Temple priests accused Jesus of saying he was a king. They said he had broken the laws of God.

They were afraid of Jesus.

They thought Jesus wanted all the people to fight against them and their Roman rulers.

The priests told him lies about Jesus. The Governor didn't want Jesus to be killed but he agreed.

The soldiers beat Jesus.

Then they made him carry a heavy cross up a hill. He was very tired and often fell down.

They nailed Jesus to a cross.

They put it up with two other crosses. Jesus's mother and his friends were there.

Jesus died at midday on Friday.

That evening, a friend called Joseph took Jesus away. He put him in a tomb on a hill.

Mary, a friend of Jesus's, went to the tomb.

It was early on Sunday morning. Mary looked in the tomb. It was empty. Jesus was gone.

Mary spoke to a man.

“Where have you taken Jesus?” she said. “Mary,” said the man. Mary saw he was Jesus.

Mary ran to tell his friends. They were very happy. They often saw Jesus before he went to Heaven.